Amazing
Monkeys

EYEWITNESS JUNIORS

Amazing Monkeys

WRITTEN BY
SCOTT STEEDMAN

PHOTOGRAPHED BY
JERRY YOUNG

ALFRED A. KNOPF • NEW YORK

Conceived and produced by
Dorling Kindersley Limited

Project editor Christine Webb
Art editor Ann Cannings
Senior art editor Jacquie Gulliver
Production Louise Barratt

Illustrations by Gill Elsbury and Julie Anderson
Animals supplied by Trevor Smith's Animal World
Editorial consultants The staff of the Natural History Museum, London

The author would like to dedicate this book to Al and Joss.

This is a Borzoi Book published by Alfred A. Knopf, Inc.

First American edition, 1991

Manufactured in Spain   0 9 8 7 6 5 4 3

Library of Congress Cataloging in Publication Data
Steedman, Scott.
Amazing monkeys / written by Scott Steedman;
photographs by Jerry Young.
p. cm. — (Eyewitness juniors)
Summary: Text and photographs focus on some of the more interesting members
of the monkey world.
1. Monkeys — Juvenile literature. 2. Primates — Juvenile literature. [1. Monkeys.]
I. Young, Jerry, ill. II. Title. III. Series.
QL737.P9S74   1991   599.8'2 — dc20   90-19238
ISBN 0-679-81517-1
ISBN 0-679-91517-6 (lib. bdg.)

Color reproduction by Colourscan, Singapore
Typeset by Windsorgraphics, Ringwood, Hampshire
Printed and bound in Spain by Artes Gráficas Toledo, S.A.
D.L. TO: 728-1996

Contents

What is a monkey?

Monkeys and apes are our closest relatives. With its big eyes and clever face, this capuchin monkey looks surprisingly human. Most amazing of all are its hands – it has delicate fingers and thumbs just like ours.

Boy   *Chimpanzee*   *Loris*   *Lemur*

The monkey family

You belong to a group of animals called primates. So do apes (including chimps) and monkeys. The only other primates are the lemurs, which look like monkeys with foxy faces, and a few tiny night animals like the loris.

Look while you leap

Leaping through the trees is a dangerous business. Monkeys and apes have big eyes which face forward, making sure they can always spy a safe landing spot *before* they reach the next tree.

Monkeying about

If you let a monkey loose in your room, it would make quite a mess. Monkeys are quick and clever, and take things apart just to see what's inside. They're a lot like people, really.

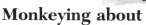

Not fussy

Fruit and flowers, birds and butterflies, bamboo shoots and crabs, eggs and frogs' legs – most monkeys will eat just about anything.

Capuchin monkey

This monkey lives in South America. It is named after capuchin monks, who wear cloaks that come down in a V-shape over their forehead – just like the brown hairs of a capuchin monkey.

Too big to swing

Most monkeys and apes swing through the treetops. But the biggest kinds move around on the ground on all fours.

Hands for gripping

Monkeys have long, strong fingers and toes. These end in nails, which don't get in the way when the monkey wraps its fingers around a branch or a banana.

9

Living together

Like people, monkeys live together. Some live in families, but other monkey societies are much bigger, with fifty or more monkeys playing, sleeping, arguing, and eating together.

Golden monkey
In the bamboo forests of China, golden monkeys live in groups, or "troops," of more than one hundred.

Look down! It's a snake!

Vervets let out different shrieks when they spot different kinds of enemies. The "eagle" alarm makes them all look up. When they hear the "leopard" alarm, they go straight up the closest tree.

Twisted tails

The titi monkey family rests cuddled together on a branch. When they go to sleep, they twine their tails together too.

Young vervet

Cleaning up your act

Many monkeys spend hours grooming – picking bugs and dirt out of each other's fur. Grooming also seems to help monkeys get along with each other.

Mother and daughter

Young monkeys stay with their mothers for a long time. This vervet monkey is two years old, but she still sticks close to Mom's side.

Mother vervet

Just like us, monkeys make faces when they're playing

You're the boss

With his tail in the air and a grin on his face, one baboon shows the sole of his foot to another. This is a strange, baboony way of saying – I admit it, you're the boss!

Leaders of the pack

In the baboon world, males are twice the size of females. Some males live on the edges of the troop, while the most important males live in the thick of the pack, surrounded by females and babies.

Funny faces

Some monkeys have the strangest looks on their faces. The cotton-top tamarin (far right) even has a hairstyle to match.

Cotton-top
This little monkey is only the size of a squirrel. It eats nuts like a squirrel, but also feeds on fruit and insects.

Who knows?
The word *proboscis* means "nose." Any idea why they call it the proboscis monkey?

Looking good
An unhealthy uakari has a pale pink face. When it is feeling well, the uakari's face turns bright red (but it doesn't get any prettier).

King of the mustaches
The emperor tamarin (left) flashes its impressive mustache at enemies, trying to appear much bigger than it really is.

Painted face
Young mandrills have dull brown faces. But when the males become adults, they get brilliant red and blue noses.

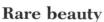

High flyer
The douc (DOOK) is one of the most agile – and beautiful – monkeys of all. With great shouts and leaps, it can throw itself 20 feet from one tree to the next. No wonder its hair stands on end!

Rare beauty
The golden marmoset has a mane like a lion. Sadly, so many have been caught and sold as pets that there are very few of them left in the wild.

Wild boy of the woods

Orangutans live in the rain forests of Indonesia and Malaysia. With their shaggy orange fur, huge arms, and pot bellies, you can see how they got their name – which is Malaysian for "wild man of the woods."

Endangered ape

Humans are the orangutan's worst enemy. So much of the rain forest has been cut down that zoos may soon be the only places to find orangs.

Stay out of my (hic) garden

To keep other orangs out of its territory, the male orangutan lets out a booming call – which ends with a series of burps and sighs.

Four hands, no feet

The orangutan's big toes work like thumbs. Its feet are so good at grasping that it seems to have four hands and no feet.

My dad's bigger than your dad

Male orangutans weigh up to 265 pounds – more than the average dad! And they're much better at hanging around in trees, too.

Fruit lover

Ripe fruit is an orangutan's favorite food. When it finds a tree full of figs or mangoes, it picks the juiciest ones and peels them carefully with its enormous fingers.

Hook-shaped hands, just right for hanging on

Still growing
This male orangutan is five years old. He won't leave his mother's side until he's seven, and won't reach his full size until he is twelve.

Where did that branch go?
By the time they've grown up, one orang in three has broken a bone by falling out of a tree!

An adult male's arms may stretch 8 feet

The fifth toe is shorter, to make it easier to swing through trees

⏰A day in the life

The morning sun finds the patas monkey waking up on a tree branch. For this big male monkey, it's the start of a long day looking after his troop.

Filling the tanks
Drinking is a dangerous business on the African plains. When the troop comes to a waterhole, the females and babies lap up all they can while the male keeps guard from a high rock or a tree stump.

An officer and a gentlemonkey
A reddish coat and impressive white mustache have given the patas another name – the military monkey.

See my teeth ?
It's easy to tell if a patas is male or female, because males are twice as big. If you're still not sure, just peel back the monkey's top lip. If it's a male, you'll find two long stabbing teeth that look like built-in knives.

The fastest primate
Long legs make the patas monkey more like a greyhound than a monkey. It can bound along at 35 miles an hour – faster than the speed limit in most cities!

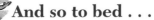

And so to bed . . .
As the sun sets on the plains, or savanna, the patas troop finds a nice big acacia tree and dozes off together.

Blooming snacks
Patas troops live
on the ground.
They spend most
of the day moving
around, looking
for leaves,
fruit, and
flowers
to eat.

The dry plains
The patas monkey is
at home on the dry
plains of Africa,
which it shares
with hyenas,
leopards,
elephants –
and more and
more people.

**I'm in
charge here**
This male
patas monkey
is five and a half
years old and fully
grown. He may be
the only grown-up male
in a troop of seven females
and ten young monkeys.

*Long legs for sprinting
across the scorching hot plains*

17

Monkeys at night

As the sun sets over the Amazon jungle, the owl monkey is just waking up. A few minutes after dark, when jaguars and eagles are safely snoring, the monkey leaves its tree hole and heads out into the night.

Owl eats owl
The only enemy the owl monkey has to fear at night is, strangely enough, the great horned owl.

Douroucouli
The owl monkey is also called by its native name, douroucouli (dor-uh-koo-lee).

Birds for breakfast
The owl monkey sneaks up and grabs birds that are sleeping quietly in their nests.

The owl monkey is the only monkey that comes out at night

Night sight

Huge eyes are just right for seeing in the dark. The owl monkey can leap from tree to tree and snatch insects out of the air, even when it's so dark that you can barely see what's in front of you.

Midnight nap

Many daytime monkeys take a nap at noon, but the owl monkey family huddles up together for a short snooze at midnight.

Bedtime

Most monkeys and apes spend the night curled up in their nests. Even the gorilla builds a nest of branches, so it won't roll down the hill in the middle of a dream.

Hooting at the moon

This monkey's sad call sounds surprisingly like the hoot of an owl. Male monkeys are the only ones that hoot, and they only seem to do it when the sky is clear and the moon is full.

Clever monkey

Macaques are fast learners. They are always trying something new. Once one macaque learns a new trick, the whole troop is soon doing it too.

Monkey culture

As we discover more about macaques, we have found out that each troop has its own way of doing things. Like French people or Chinese people, macaque troops have their own culture.

Exotic tastes

The crab-eating macaque lives by rivers, where it fishes for – you guessed it – crabs.

Holy monkeys

The Buddhist monks of Nepal take good care of macaques, feeding them and letting them climb all over the temple roofs.

Hot tub

In the high mountains of Japan, macaques keep warm by taking a dip in hot volcanic pools while the snow falls around them.

Can I pay in bananas?

In Malaysia, pig-tailed macaques are trained to climb palm trees and pick ripe coconuts. Every day they are paid for their work – in bananas!

The clever ape

Tame chimpanzees have learned to speak in sign language. And in the wild, they learn to use sticks to trick ants out of anthills.

A wash before dinner

Once, a macaque called Imo discovered that if she washed her sweet potato before eating it, she wouldn't get sand in her mouth. Six months later, Imo's whole troop was cleaning its potatoes too.

Crab-eating macaque
Macaques are found in Africa and in Asia from Tibet to Indonesia. The crab-eating macaque lives near swamps and rivers all over Southeast Asia.

Macaques have a frill of hair around their face

Like us, macaques can pick up the tiniest object with their fingers and thumb

Macaques live in trees and on the ground

21

Monkey talk

High in the jungle treetops, monkeys shout and squeak to keep in touch. Their calls may say "Come quick! I've found some mangoes." Or they may just mean "Keep out of my home."

Singsong

Gibbon couples don't just live together, they also sing together. If the mother is carrying a baby, the baby will often try to join the chorus too.

Whoop-gobble

Male mangabey monkeys make great "whoop-gobble" calls. Next time you're in Zaire, listen out for them – they sound just like Tarzan's famous call (but louder).

Talking back

The face isn't the only part of the body that talks. When female hamadryas baboons are ready for romance, they signal to the males with their bottoms, which swell and get bright red.

Scared

Playful

Sad

Making faces
Chimpanzees flash their teeth when they're scared, and laugh when they want to play. When they're sad, they seem to cry.

Know any Mozart?
Many monkeys can shriek louder than the loudest opera singer.

Calling the bluff
When two male gorillas meet in the forest, they bark, roar, tear up the shrubbery, and beat their chests. Usually the smaller one backs off before a fight starts and he gets hurt.

Canary of the jungle
The tiny marmoset (left) whistles and squeaks. When marmosets move through the Brazilian jungle, they chatter away like a flock of birds.

The monkey family

Monkeys and apes aren't the only primates. There are 181 different kinds, from bushbabies that look like wide-eyed possums to the most common primate of all – you.

Living on an island
The strange and beautiful lemur is found only on the African island of Madagascar. As it runs along the ground, it looks like a cross between a raccoon and a monkey.

The amazing aye-aye
Experts used to think the aye-aye was a weird squirrel with huge ears. But now they know it is really a lemur.
Its fingers are incredibly long and skinny, especially the middle ones, which it uses for prying grubs out of logs.

Gorillas and mice
The biggest primate, the male gorilla, weighs as much as 450 pounds. That's three times heavier than an average person – and three thousand times heavier than the smallest primate, the gray mouse lemur.

Bushbabies
The bushbaby and the tarsier are small primates that only come out at night. They may look like the first primates, which appeared when dinosaurs still roamed the earth.

Tarsier

Bushbaby

De Brazza's monkey
This monkey (below) is at home in the swampy forests of Central Africa. It is a typical monkey, long-tailed and very curious.

Long, strong arms and legs make running and bounding easy work

Naked ape
You may wear nice shirts and study with a computer. But under your clothing, you are an animal. Humans just have bigger brains, and less hair, than monkeys and apes.

Growing up

A baby gibbon spends its first years clinging to its mother's fur. It has to hang on tight, because she moves fast, and the jungle floor is a long way down.

Living bridge
A baby spider monkey has problems crossing big gaps between two trees. The mother helps out by stretching her body into a living bridge which the little one can scramble across.

Tightrope champ
The gibbon is famous for its tightrope walking. A mother will run gracefully along a branch, with her long arms out for balance and her baby clinging tight to her belly.

Piggyback
When they get a bit older, young monkeys and apes start riding around on Mom's (or even Dad's) back. Soon they will start to spend more time away from her side.

Mother's milk
Like a human, a monkey baby starts drinking its mother's milk from the day it's born. For the first few months it rarely leaves the breast, where a nipple is always close by.

Warning! Fragile
Their mothers are dull gray, but baby leaf monkeys are a bright apricot color. This bold coloring makes older monkeys treat the babies with extra special care.

Playing house
A young chimp spends hours "helping" and copying its mother as she builds a nest for the night. When it finally has to make its own nest, it has a pretty good idea of what to do.

Busy parents
A baby gibbon is born to a gibbon couple every two or three years. It won't leave home until it's eight years old.

This baby gibbon is only one month old

Amazing grace

Monkeys are the acrobats of the animal world. They are fast and graceful, and make bounding through the trees look as easy as walking down the street.

King of the swingers
The agile gibbon swings along beneath the branches, hanging on with hands like muscular hooks.

Can monkeys fly?

No primate gets around by flying, gliding, hopping, or digging. But a few, like the proboscis monkey, can dive into the water and swim away from danger.

... and a tail makes five

Using its strong tail like an extra arm, the spider monkey can hang from a branch and still have two hands for eating.

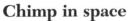

Chimp in space

One of the first apes in space was Ham the chimpanzee. He spent 16 minutes spinning above the Earth at nearly 5,000 miles per hour – wearing a special pressurized chimp suit, of course.

Knuckle walkers

Gorillas and chimpanzees walk on all fours. They plunk their feet flat on the ground, but curl their fingers over and walk on the knuckles of their hands.

Black spider monkey

Stretched out between jungle branches, this Brazilian monkey looks like a huge, hairy spider.

Index